A real sleepover party!

"Birthday? Since when do vampires celebrate birthdays? Everyone knows vampires are undead."

Drak clutched his glass. "I know, I know. We aren't alive and we aren't dead. But I've never had a birthday party before and it sounds like a lot of fun."

Mrs. Fangula tapped her long, red fingernails on her glass. "I don't think so, Drak. When could we do it? I'm asleep during the day."

"That's why I thought we could have a slumber party," Drak explained. "At night."

"Still . . . All that fresh blood running around the house. All those humans."

"I just want to fit in, Mom," said Drak. "That's why I want a birthday party. How about it, Mom. Please?"

Mrs. Fangula hesitated. "You'll have to promise to eat before your guests arrive."

"I promise! I promise!" Drak said, hopping up and down.

Mrs. Fangula smiled. "A birthday party for a vampire," she said, shaking her head. "What will you think of next!"

Don't miss any of the books in this great new series!

Drak's Slumber Party
*Frank's Field Trip**
*Harry Goes to Camp**

* coming soon

MONSTERKIDS

Drak's Slumber Party

by Gertrude Gruesome

HarperPaperbacks
A Division of HarperCollins*Publishers*

This is a work of fiction. The characters, incidents, and dialogues are products of the author's imagination and are not to be construed as real. Any resemblance to actual events or persons, living or dead, is entirely coincidental.

HarperPaperbacks *A Division of* HarperCollins*Publishers*
10 East 53rd Street, New York, N.Y. 10022

A Creative Media Applications Book
Written by: Paige McBrier
Editor: Susan Freeman
Art Direction: Fabia Wargin

Cover Art: Greg Wrey
Interior Art: Glen Hanson

First HarperPaperbacks printing: January 1995

Printed in the United States of America

HarperPaperbacks and colophon are trademarks of HarperCollins*Publishers*

❖ 10 9 8 7 6 5 4 3 2 1

Reprinted by arrangement with HarperPaperbacks,
a division of Harper Collins Publishers.

Drak's Slumber Party

CHAPTER One

"Wake up, Mom. I'm home!" Drak Fangula tossed his sunglasses and book bag onto the floor and hurried down the long, steep stairway to the cellar, two steps at a time. He had something major to ask his mother today.

In the cellar, Mr. and Mrs. Fangula were still sleeping soundly in their matching mahogany coffins. Drak tiptoed across the stone floor, then politely leaned over his mother's coffin. He smiled his most friendly smile. "Hi, Mom," he said, whispering softly so as not to wake his father. "Time to get up!"

Mrs. Fangula slowly opened her glassy red eyes. She blinked. "What time is it?"

"Five thirty in the afternoon," Drak answered. "Almost dark."

Mrs. Fangula sat up. "Oh, no! I must have overslept again." She sighed. "I'll never get used to these early hours."

Drak and his parents were vampires, and most vampires sleep during the day because sunlight bothers them. Now that Drak's family was living among humans, though, they'd had to make some changes.

The biggest change for Drak was school, which now started at eight in the morning instead of eight at night. And for Drak, getting used to the sunlight had been especially hard. He'd had to get special permission from the school nurse to wear sunglasses during class.

At first it felt a little funny to be the only kid in school with fangs and sunglasses. As far as Drak knew, he was the only vampire ever to attend Pearson Elementary. He had sort of worried about it in the beginning, especially when one of the boys made a dumb joke about needing Drak's fangs to unclog the glue cap. But Drak's teacher, Mrs. Love, had overheard and reminded the kid that "at Pearson Elementary we're all special because we're all different."

Since then, everyone had accepted him for who he was. And now that he had made a few friends and started dressing more like a human, no one seemed to notice his fangs anymore. Maybe they just thought he needed braces.

Mrs. Fangula yawned. She squinted at the daylight coming in from underneath her heavy curtains. She rubbed her eyes and frowned. "Drak, *what* are you wearing?"

Drak tugged on his shirt. "It's my new T-shirt, Mom. Remember? I told you I got it yesterday when I was with Jeremy."

His mother leaned forward to read the lettering. "'Surf Doggies?'" she said. "What's that supposed to mean?"

"I don't know," Drak said. "I think it's surfer words."

Mrs. Fangula sighed and climbed out of her coffin. "A surfing vampire," she said. "What next?" She put on her long red bathrobe cape and stepped into a pair of matching slippers. "I guess I'm old-fashioned, but I still think there's nothing nicer than a starched white shirt and a long black cape."

Drak didn't answer. Instead he quietly followed his mother down the stairs and into the kitchen. Ordinarily he *would* have said something. Nobody at Pearson Elementary would be caught dead in a cape unless they were appearing in "Little Red Riding Hood." But not today. Today he needed his mother to be in a good mood.

Mrs. Fangula walked over to the refrigerator and opened the door. Inside, pitchers of blood labeled TYPE A, TYPE B, and TYPE O sat neatly on the top shelf. "What can I get you for a snack?" she asked.

"How about an AB shake?" Drak said.

His mother nodded. "Sounds good. I think I'll have one too. I could use a little extra protein today."

Like most vampires, Drak's family drank blood. Lots of it. Once a month Drak's mother put in an order at the blood bank for six gallons each of Types A, B, O, and AB. She believed the blood bank was a more civilized way of eating.

Mrs. Fangula pulled the blender out from underneath the sink. "So, tell me about your day."

"We started a new science project," Drak said. Drak was in the third grade this year. "Jeremy and I are making an exploding volcano."

"Sounds like fun," his mother said. "When I was in the third grade, we blew up the teacher for our science project."

Drak gasped. "What happened to him?"

TYPE A
TYPE B
TYPE O
TYPE AB
SURF DOGGIE

"He gave us an A," she said. She handed Drak his bloodshake. "When are we going to meet this Jeremy?"

Drak saw his chance to bring up the question he wanted to ask. "I've been meaning to talk to you about that. Did you know my birthday is coming up in two weeks?" He took a nervous gulp of his drink.

Mrs. Fangula raised her eyebrows. "Birthday? Since when do vampires celebrate birthdays? Everyone knows vampires are undead."

Drak clutched his glass. "I know, I know. We aren't alive and we aren't dead. But I've never had a birthday party before, and it sounds like a lot of fun. Besides, there's a bunch of kids from my class who want to come see our castle." He gulped down some more of his shake.

Mrs. Fangula tapped her long red fingernails on her glass. "I don't think so, Drak. When could we do it? I'm asleep during the day."

"That's why I thought we could have a slumber party," Drak explained. "At night. We could start around eight o'clock, after Dad leaves for work." Drak's father sang with a band called the Lounge Lizards. They specialized in corny love ballads like "Can I Get an Itty Bitty Bite

Tonight?" and "What the Heck, I Love Your Neck!"

"Can we do it, Mom? Please?" Drak begged. "It's only a few extra kids for the night."

Mrs. Fangula raised her eyebrows. "How *many* extra?"

"Maybe eight?" said Drak.

"Eight!"

"Or seven, or six . . ."

"Five," said his mother firmly. Then she shook her head. "Still . . . all that fresh blood running around the house. All those humans." She ruffled her fingers through his red hair. "What *did* you do to your hair today, Drak?"

"I put gel in it."

"It's standing straight up."

"That's the style, Mom."

"You look like a warlock."

Drak rolled his eyes. He could feel his mother studying him.

"Are you glad we decided to move to New Jersey?"

"Definitely," said Drak.

"I wanted you to have a normal upbringing," she went on. "Transylvania has become so violent. Too many monsters for such a small spot. Things are so peaceful here. We were lucky enough to find this castle in a good neighborhood. You go to a nice school. The blood bank is just around the corner . . . " She squinted. "But you *are* starting to look more human."

"I just want to fit in, Mom," said Drak. "That's why I want a birthday party."

"I know." Mrs. Fangula handed him a napkin. "If you're finished, please wipe that blood off your mouth."

"How about it, Mom. Please?"

Mrs. Fangula hesitated. "You'll have to promise to eat before your guests arrive."

"I promise! I promise!" Drak said, hopping up and down.

"And you'll have to make sure there's plenty for your friends to do until they fall asleep."

"Okay," Drak said.

Mrs. Fangula smiled. "A birthday party for a vampire," she said, shaking her head. "What will you think of next!"

CHAPTER Two

Drak couldn't wait to get to school the next day to tell Jeremy.

"She said *yes*," he told Jeremy the minute he saw him come through the school's front doors.

"Yes!" said Jeremy, slapping his hand. "Drak, you are going to love having a slumber party. They are so much fun. You get to stay up late, have pillow fights, and eat a lot of junk food."

"I know, I know," Drak said. "You told me." He and Jeremy headed for Mrs. Love's room. Jeremy was the first best friend Drak had ever had. He had dark curly hair and a friendly smile. He also knew how to skateboard and had a real trampoline in his backyard.

"So who are you going to invite to your party?" Jeremy asked.

"I don't know. Mom said I could ask five kids."

"Five! Wow!" The last bell rang and Jeremy slid into his seat. "We can talk more at recess, okay?"

"Great!" Drak said.

As soon as lunch was over, Drak and Jeremy hurried to the playground. When they got outside, they made a run for the nearest group of shady trees.

A bunch of girls were there practicing cheers. "Hey! We were here first," said Jennifer Lockett.

"Drak can't be out in the sun, remember?" Jeremy said.

"It's okay," said Drak. "We can go under those other trees." He hated to make a big deal about himself.

After they finally settled down, Jeremy took out his notebook and a pencil. "Let's start with the guest list. Who do you want to ask? You have space for four more people."

Drak watched some boys from his class playing on the slide. "How about Brendan, Chris, and Steven?"

"Sounds good," said Jeremy, writing down their names. "One more."

PEARSON ELEME
SURF
OGGIE

Drak's eyes moved across the playground. "What about Doug?"

"Yeah! Doug!" Jeremy said. Everybody liked Doug. He was the funniest kid in school. He was always telling jokes and making weird faces.

"Now for the games," Jeremy said. "What games do you have at your house?"

"We have a video game."

"Okay, that's one. Do you have any good board games?"

"Not really," Drak said. "Unless you count the Ouija board." His mother was an expert at that.

"That counts," Jeremy said. "And we can do stuff like hide-and-seek and tag. *And* don't forget presents. Now what kind of food do you want?"

"Food?"

"Yeah. Chips, ice cream, Fruit Roll-Ups, cookies . . . the good stuff."

"I don't know," Drak said. "We're not big eaters."

"That's right. I forgot," Jeremy said. When Drak first told Jeremy that all he ever had in his lunch thermos was blood, Jeremy was very nice about it. He told Drak that sometimes he wished he could just have milkshakes for lunch.

"Don't worry about the food, Drak," Jeremy said. "As long it has lots of sugar or salt, everyone will love it. I can go to the store with you and help pick out some things."

"That'd be great!" Drak said. He remembered something else. "What will people sleep on?"

"Everyone brings a pillow and sleeping bag," Jeremy told him.

"That's good," Drak said. All they had were coffins.

"Now what kind of birthday cake are you going to have?" Jeremy asked.

Drak stopped. "My mother doesn't cook."

"No problem," Jeremy said, waving his hand. "I'll ask my mother to make the cake. She won't mind."

"Are you sure?" said Drak.

"Positive. What kind do you want?"

Drak thought for a minute. "How about white on the outside and red on the inside?"

"Okay," said Jeremy. He carefully wrote down all the information. When he finished, he said, "I can tell this is going to be a great party."

"Why?"

"Well, for one thing, you're the only kid in the third grade who lives in a castle."

Drak shrugged modestly. "Mom says it needs a lot of work."

"I can't wait to see your house," Jeremy went on. "We can play tag and tell spooky stories and do all kinds of fun stuff. A castle is the perfect place for a slumber party."

Drak smiled. "That's exactly what I told my Mom."

CHAPTER Three

Drak stood in the kitchen, staring at a container of sour-cream dip. The night of his birthday party had finally arrived, and he was busy with last-minute preparations. Now what was it Jeremy had said? The sour-cream dip went with the Oreos? Or was it sour cream and chips?

He moved the bag of chips next to the Oreos. No . . . maybe the other way around was better. He'd never get used to human food.

"Ready for the party?" asked Drak's father, coming into the room. He was dressed for work. He had on a long black cape, a white tuxedo shirt and tails, and shiny patent-leather shoes. His dark hair was slicked back, and his two fangs — the left longer than the right — glowed in the dark.

CHIPS
FRUIT ROLL-UPS

"I'm having trouble figuring out what food goes with what," Drak said.

His father studied the food lineup. There were chips, Oreos, sour-cream dip, Fruit Roll-Ups, popcorn, and pretzels. "The popcorn gets dipped in the sour cream and the Fruit Roll-Ups go around the pretzels," he said.

"Are you sure?"

"Positive." Mr. Fangula opened the refrigerator, poured himself a glass of Type O, and drank it down. He practiced a few scales to warm up his voice. "Me, me, me, me," he sang. He had another glass of O. "Me, me, me, me," he repeated. Then, still singing, he said, "Drak, when are your friends coming?"

"In about fifteen minutes," Drak answered in his normal voice. He hoped his father would be warmed up and gone by then. He hadn't told anyone that his father was a lounge singer. It was bad enough that they were vampires. When Jeremy had asked what his father did, Drak told him he worked in the post office.

Mrs. Fangula came into the kitchen. "Drak, is everything ready?"

"Cosima, you look spectacular!" said Mr. Fangula. He started in on one of his love ballads.

Mrs. Fangula blushed, and shushed him up. "Thank you, Vladimir. I wanted to look nice for Drak's party." She had on a fiery red-and-black satin cape over a tight-fitting black dress. Her long dark hair was piled up on top of her head.

"I thought you were going to wear your white dress," said Drak. "And no cape."

"This is more festive," his mother said. She eyed him up and down but didn't say anything about *his* outfit — jeans, a T-shirt, and red high-top sneakers.

Drak's father cleared his throat. "I'm sorry to miss the party."

"We're sorry too, Vlad," said his mother. "Remember all those wonderful parties we used to have back in Transylvania? Everyone was there . . . the witches, the warlocks, the werewolves. People talked about those parties for days afterward."

Drak's mother poured two glasses of blood, one for herself and one for Drak. "To your party, Drak," she said, giving him a toast. "Let's hope everything goes all right." She drained her glass of blood. "Whew. I was thirsty after sleeping all day! I think I'll have another." She looked at Drak. "You should too, dear. I don't want you getting hungry later."

"Mom, stop worrying," Drak said. "These are my friends."

His mother poured him a tall glass. "Drink," she said.

Drak's father took his mother's hands. "Cosima, everything will be fine. Drak's friends will run around, eat too much, then fall asleep. I see it happen all the time with humans." He kissed her hands. "See you in the morning, my beloved." He turned to Drak. "Happy birthday, son."

"Thanks. Bye, Dad."

As soon as Drak's father left, his mother turned to him and said, "Have you cleaned all the cobwebs in the library?" They'd decided to hold the party in the library since it had a fireplace and plenty of room for sleeping bags.

"Done," Drak said.

"Is the fire lit?"

"Yep."

"How about this food? Doesn't it belong in the library?"

"I wanted Jeremy to see it first," said Drak. "In case it's not right."

Mrs. Fangula nodded. "Well, I guess we're set. Now remember. I don't want anyone playing with the tarantula or going down into my dungeon."

Drak grinned. "Okay, Mom. Wait! I just remembered the candles." Drak's family didn't use electric light in their castle because vampires can see in the dark.

Drak ran to the library and carefully lit the giant silver candelabras. He had just finished when he heard a car pull into the driveway.

"They're here!" he said. He ran to the window and peered out.

A banged-up old car—the kind they use for funerals—drove up to the front door. Drak scratched his head. He hadn't remembered any of his friends saying anything about a hearse.

Then he heard a horribly familiar laugh. The hairs on the back of his neck stood up straight.

"Oh, no," said Drak. "Oh, no! Not them!"

He stared out the window. A family of badly dressed vampires came spilling out of the car. They were all there. Uncle Mort, Aunt Esther, and his cousins Ella, Margaret, and Vincent.

Drak slumped against the window and groaned. "Mom!" he yelled. "Who invited the Chompulas?"

CHAPTER Four

Drak's mother rushed to his side. "What are *they* doing here?"

They ran into the hall just as the front door flew open.

"Surprise!" yelled Uncle Mort.

"You can't stay," Drak blurted out. "I'm having a slumber party tonight. I've invited five friends from my human school."

"Terrific!" said Uncle Mort. "I'm starved." He turned around and hollered, "Come on in, kids."

"But . . . " said Drak.

He and his mother watched helplessly as Aunt Esther and the kids pushed their way inside. The Chompulas didn't know the meaning of the word "polite." They were loud, rude, and obnoxious.

Uncle Mort threw his arms around Drak's mother. "How's my baby sister?" he said.

Drak wrinkled his nose. Uncle Mort's breath smelled like a dead squirrel. His tuxedo shirt was dirty and stained. His cape needed to be ironed.

"What are you doing here, Mortimer?" Drak's mother asked.

"We wanted to see your new home," Uncle Mort said.

"And we haven't heard from you since you left Transylvania," added Aunt Esther. "Not even a phone call."

"Oh, well . . . we've been so busy," said Drak's mother.

"Looks like you've put on some weight, Cosima," Aunt Esther said. "It must be that bottled blood. Why don't you come home to Transylvania?"

"We're very happy here," Drak's mother said. "Vladimir has a good job singing at the Starlight Club, and Drak has made lots of new friends at school."

Drak glanced nervously out the front door. What was he going to do? His guests would be here any minute. Aunt Esther patted him on the head. "I see you're dressing like a human now, Drak."

"What do you expect?" Drak muttered under his breath.

Ella and Margaret came through the front door again, dragging a pair of scratched-up coffins. Ella was tall like her father and had stringy dark hair. Margaret looked more like Aunt Esther, short and wide. They both wore long wrinkled dresses and capes.

"Where are you going with those coffins?" asked Drak. "Leave them in the car. I'm about to have a party!"

"We heard," Ella said. "Will there be boys?"

"No," said Drak. "I mean, yes. But none for you."

Ella and Margaret giggled and started dragging their coffins toward the library.

"Wait! Stop! You're going to wreck my party."

"No we're not," said Ella. "We love parties."

Drak followed them into the library. "But you don't understand," he said desperately. The girls ignored him.

On the other side of the room, Drak's younger cousin Vincent examined the wires on the video game. He sniffed them, then put them between his teeth. "Stop!" yelled Drak.

Vincent chomped down. The wires snapped in half, shooting off a string of sparks. Vincent's red hair stood on end. "Wow," he said.

"Mom," yelled Margaret. "Vincent's playing with fire again." Vincent threw the wires onto the floor.

Drak rushed over. "Vincent! Why did you do that? You ruined my video game! We were going to use it during the party."

Vincent turned himself into a black cat and hissed at Drak. Vampires are able to change themselves into bats, cats, or puffs of smoke, tricks that Drak hardly ever used. He didn't like to show off.

Suddenly Drak heard growling behind him. He spun around and saw Margaret ripping the couch pillows apart with her fangs.

"Margaret! No!" The feathers from the pillows flew all over the room. The more feathers, the more excited Margaret became. Feathers were stuck in her hair and on her clothing. Several clung to the sides of her mouth.

"Margaret, stop! What are you doing?" Drak yelled.

"She's looking for chickens," Ella explained.

"She smelled the feathers and had a craving for chicken blood."

"But there aren't any chickens in there," shouted Drak. "We were going to use those pillows for the pillow fight. Now what am I supposed to do?"

Vincent, still a cat, started batting the feathers around the room.

Drak ran to the window and looked out. "My friends will be here any minute. Vincent, you can't be a cat when my guests arrive. They won't understand."

Vincent yawned. He began licking his paws.

Drak picked him up by the neck. "I mean it, Vincent."

Vincent hissed.

"Mom," yelled Margaret. "Vincent's being obnoxious again."

Ella said, "Can I see your room, Drak?"

"No."

Ella started up the stairs anyway.

"No one is allowed in my room," Drak said, running after her.

They met his mother and aunt Esther and uncle Mort standing on the stairs. "You should see what the Orlocks have done to your old castle,"

Aunt Esther was saying to his mother. "You would hardly recognize it."

"Mom!" said Drak, interrupting them. "The library is a mess and it's eight o'clock and any second now . . . "

The doorbell rang.

Drak froze.

"Dinner!" warbled Aunt Esther. "Come and get it, kids!"

CHAPTER Five

The Chompulas rushed to the door.

Drak and his mother tore after them. "No, wait," said Drak, throwing himself in front of them. "These guys don't taste good."

"Nonsense," said Uncle Mort, shoving him aside. "Your mother wouldn't serve anything that wasn't wonderful."

Drak's mother threw out her arm and blocked his path. "Mortimer Chompula, you stop right there!" Behind Uncle Mort, the rest of the Chompulas kept pushing and shoving.

"Enough!" yelled Drak's mother. Vincent, still a cat, threaded himself between her legs. "Vincent, no cats tonight." He changed back to himself, a little vampire with a runny nose.

Drak and his mother stood with their backs to

the front door. Mrs. Fangula looked sternly at the Chompulas. "Now, this is Drak's party and no one is going to spoil it, understand? I expect all of you to keep your fangs out of the guests. You're welcome to help yourself to whatever is in the fridge."

The Chompulas quieted down.

Mrs. Fangula took a deep breath, put on a big smile, and opened the door. "Greetings!" she said.

Jeremy and his mother stood outside. Mrs. Muniz was holding Drak's birthday cake. She smiled weakly. "Are we interrupting anything?"

"No," said Drak and his mother in unison.

"Come right in," said Mrs. Fangula. "I'm Cosima Fangula, Drak's mother. We've heard a lot of nice things about Jeremy."

Mrs. Muniz stared at the inside of the castle. Then she turned back and stared at the Chompulas' hearse.

Jeremy, who had been looking around the front hall, said, "Wow! Your house is cool, Drak!"

The Chompulas, still clustered by the stairs, laughed nervously.

Mrs. Muniz saw them and went pale.

Mrs. Fangula cleared her throat. "I'd like you

HAPPY BIRTHDAY DRAK

to meet my brother Mortimer and his family," she said politely. "They're visiting us for the evening."

"Pleased to meet you," whispered Mrs. Muniz.

"Did you notice my cake, Mom?" said Drak, trying to change the subject. It looked just as Drak had hoped it would. It had white icing and nine candles and said HAPPY BIRTHDAY, DRAK in red letters.

"It's lovely," said Drak's mother to Mrs. Muniz.

"It's cherry inside," Mrs. Muniz said.

Aunt Esther leaned forward. "Drak is having a *birthday party*, Cosima?" she asked. "Since when do vam— "

"May I take that cake into the kitchen?" Mrs. Fangula interrupted.

Mrs. Muniz gripped the pan.

"Let me put that down for you," said Mrs. Fangula, politely tugging.

The doorbell rang a second time. As Drak opened the heavy door, Chris Rogers and Doug Wilson raced inside. "Wow! What a place," said Doug. He tossed his sleeping bag on the floor and gave Drak his gift.

"Cool!" said Chris, dropping his stuff and heading up the stairs. "Come on," he yelled from the top. "Who wants to slide down the railing with me?"

"I do," said Jeremy. He turned to his mother. "You can go now, Mom." He bolted upstairs.

Mrs. Muniz wrung her hands.

"He'll be fine," said Mrs. Fangula, taking the cake from her.

"Good-bye, Jeremy," his mother called. She turned to leave.

Uncle Mort swiftly glided up behind her. "Good to eat—I mean, *meet* you," he said, leaning over her neck. His mouth cranked open.

"Mrs. Muniz! Wait!" said Drak.

Mrs. Muniz spun around. Uncle Mort stepped back.

"Uh, I forgot to thank you for the cake," Drak said.

"Don't mention it. I love to bake," she called quickly and slipped out the door.

As soon as Drak's mother shut the door, she gave Uncle Mort a dirty look. "You should be ashamed."

"I couldn't help it, Cosima," he said. "I got a whiff of Type A."

"There's plenty of A in the refrigerator," she answered.

"But Cosima," said Aunt Esther. "There's nothing like fresh A. You know that. I hate that bottled stuff."

Drak's mother didn't say anything.

The doorbell rang again. It was Brendan and Steven. "Happy birthday, Drak," they said, handing him their presents.

"We're up here, Brendan," Chris called from the top of the stairs.

The boys dropped their things and headed up. As Steven ran past Ella, she said, "Type B. Mmmm."

Uncle Mort had his nose in the air. "Esther," he said. "Did you catch that whiff of A negative?"

"Delicious," she said. The Chompulas were still pressed together, loudly sniffing. Every time one of Drak's friends slid past them on the banister, they tried to smell his blood type.

"That's an AB," said Margaret as Chris slid past.

"No, it's not," said Ella. "It's an O."

Drak looked at his friends racing down the banister. Then he looked at the Chompulas, sniffing away. He needed to get their minds off food.

"How about a game of charades, everyone?" he said.

CHAPTER Six

Drak cupped his hands around his mouth. "Everybody to the library," he announced. "Charades begins in one minute."

Steven flew off the end of the stair railing, barely missing the Chompulas. "Is there food in there?" he asked. Steven was a big eater. He looked like a sixth grader.

Ella leaned in close. "There's food everywhere, Steven."

"I'll bring out the refreshments," said Drak's mother. "Drak, show your guests to the library. Mortimer and Esther, come with me."

"Thanks, Mom," said Drak. He kept his eyes on his cousins as everyone raced into the library.

"Wow!" said Doug. "Cool decorations! Candles, a fireplace, coffins. And look at all those feathers. Hey, guys! Let's have a feather fight!" He ran over and started tossing feathers in the air. Steven joined him.

"Can we sleep in the coffins tonight?" asked Chris.

"I don't think so . . . " Drak started to say.

Jeremy and Brendan were already arguing over Margaret's beat-up old coffin.

"I saw it first," said Brendan.

"But I got here first," said Jeremy.

"Did not."

"Did too."

"Let's move over here for charades," said Drak, waving his arms by the sofa.

No one seemed to be listening.

Vincent slid up beside Chris. "Wanna try out my coffin? It's in the corner."

"Sure," said Chris.

Vincent led him over. "Climb in," he said. His beady red eyes glittered. "It's very cozy in there."

"Looks nice," joked Chris. Drak watched him step inside.

"Now, lie down, close your eyes, and pretend you're asleep," said Vincent. "Nighty-night." He licked his lips.

"Uh-oh," said Drak from across the room.

Vincent leaned over. His mouth stretched wide.

Drak rushed over. He slammed the coffin lid down just in time.

"Yeow! My fingers!" screamed Vincent, hopping up and down.

The coffin lid popped back open. "Drak!" said Chris. "What are you trying to do? Kill someone?"

Drak's heart was pounding. "No. I, uh . . . sorry. Are you okay, Vincent?"

He nodded and sucked his sore fingers.

"Let's play charades now," said Drak.

He got everyone to sit on the two couches by the fireplace. "I'm captain," said Margaret.

"So am I," said Ella.

They chose up sides. "That B in the corner," Ella pointed.

"Who, me?" said Steven.

"I want the A negative," said Margaret. "The cute one with glasses."

Doug rolled his eyes.

Once everyone was picked, it was time to play. "I'm going first," said Margaret.

The other team handed her the name of a book to act out: *The Cat in the Hat*.

Margaret held up five fingers.

"Five words," said Doug.

Margaret nodded and held up two fingers and then five fingers.

"Second word and fifth word," said Doug.

Margaret tugged on her ear.

"Sounds like . . . " said Jeremy.

Margaret suddenly changed into a bat.

"Uh-oh," Drak said again.

Margaret's beady red eyes fixed on Jeremy and Doug. She charged.

"Mom, Margaret's hungry," called Vincent.

Margaret's wings beat fast. Her pudgy mouth opened up, revealing sharp white teeth.

"Watch out!" called Drak.

Just as Margaret swooped down on Jeremy, he jumped up. "I know! I know!" he said, waving his arms.

Boom! He knocked Margaret clear across the room. "It's a bat! Right?"

Margaret changed back. She nodded and rubbed her forehead. A big lump had started.

"Bat . . . cat . . . hat . . . *The Cat in the Hat*!" said Jeremy.

"You got it," said Margaret. She limped back to the couch.

URF
OGGIES

"Your cousins are amazing," Doug whispered into Drak's ear. "Are all vampires good actors?"

"Maybe we should play something else," Drak suggested. "Something more quiet."

"How about hide-and-seek?" said Chris. "I'm it."

Drak pictured his cousins on the loose. "That's a little *too* quiet," he said.

"Why?" said Brendan. "Look at all the places to hide in here."

"Yeah!" said Steven. "We could get lost forever."

"I like that idea," said Ella.

Drak looked around wildly. "I don't."

Chris covered his eyes and started counting. "One, two, three . . . "

"Wait . . . " Drak said.

But everyone had already scattered.

Uncle Mort and Aunt Esther walked in carrying baskets of popcorn and tortilla chips. "Oh, goody," said Uncle Mort. "Hide-and-seek." He tiptoed after Jeremy.

Drak reached out to stop him. As he grabbed Uncle Mort's arm, the basket of popcorn spilled onto the floor.

Right away, Uncle Mort forgot about Jeremy and dropped to his knees. He started counting the popcorn kernels, one by one. Aunt Esther joined in.

Drak took a deep breath. How could he have forgotten? Whenever someone scatters grain or kernels on the ground, a vampire must count every kernel he sees.

Drak quickly closed his eyes so he wouldn't have to count and poured the rest of the popcorn onto the ground. That would keep Aunt Esther and Uncle Mort busy for a while.

"Ready or not, here I come," called Chris.

Drak raced down the hall and ducked into the dining room. He glanced around. No vampires in here. He headed for the living room. Any second he expected to hear a scream from somewhere in the castle.

The living room looked empty. Then, in the corner near some tall windows, Drak noticed Steven poking his head out from behind a huge potted plant. Ella sneaked up behind him. Her arms lifted high. Her lips curled back. She moved in for the kill.

"Psst! Steven!" said Drak.

Steven jumped up. "Who's there?" He crashed into Ella who was bent over his neck, and they both fell backward.

"Oomph!"

Drak rushed over to untangle them. "Are you okay?" he asked.

"I think so," said Steven.

"He landed on my foot," said Ella, rubbing her ankle.

"Lucky for you, Ella," hissed Drak under his breath. "Why don't you go get a snack in the *kitchen,* instead?" Ella gave Drak a dirty look and stomped off.

Steven winked at Drak. "I think she likes me."

"I can tell," said Drak.

"Really?" said Steven. He gazed at the doorway.

Drak picked himself up.

"Where are you going?" asked Steven.

"I want to make sure Ella finds the kitchen," said Drak.

CHAPTER
Seven

The only person Drak found in the kitchen was his mother, who was busy thawing frozen blood in the microwave.

"Mom! What are you doing?" he asked. "This is no time to be defrosting blood."

"I can't help it," his mother said. "Mort and Esther drank every last drop we had in the fridge. Do you believe it?"

"No," said Drak. "Especially since Uncle Mort just tried to eat Jeremy."

Drak's mother shook her head. "Oh, honestly. People like Mort and Esther give vampires a bad name. They have no morals. None."

Drak nodded. "You're right. And if we don't do something soon, I'm going to start losing party guests."

"I know, I know," said Drak's mother. She handed Drak a half-frozen container of B. "Stir this up for me, will you?" She ran over to the cabinets and began rummaging through the drawers.

"What are you doing, Mom?"

"Looking for the silver knives," she said.

Drak glanced nervously out the door. To kill a vampire, you must first drive a silver stake through its heart.

"Why?"

Mrs. Fangula looked up. "Because if your friends sleep on top of silver knives, vampires can't hurt them, dear."

"Mom, by bedtime I'll be lucky if I still *have* any friends."

Mrs. Fangula slammed the drawer shut. "You're right," she said. "This is awful. Your first party, and it's about to be ruined. Maybe it was a mistake for me to think we'd be happy among humans."

"Mom . . . "

Out of the corner of his eye, Drak noticed a small black cat slip into the kitchen.

"Vincent!" yelled Drak. "Grow up!"

Vincent hissed and ran out of the room.

"Why'd you do that?" said his mother. "We could have fed him a saucer of blood."

"All the blood in the world isn't going to stop the Chompulas from attacking," said Drak.

"You're right," said his mother. "We have to get rid of them. But how?"

Drak squeezed his eyes shut and tried to think. Suddenly he had an idea. It was a long shot, but maybe . . . He whispered his idea to his mother.

Mrs. Fangula beamed. "You think that'd work?"

"I hope so."

"So do I." His mother pushed him toward the door. "Go call," she said. "You can use the phone in our room."

"I'll be right back," said Drak.

Downstairs, Drak worked fast. He looked up the phone number he needed and made his call. Two minutes later, he was on his way back upstairs.

Drak felt proud. He'd figured out a plan. A good plan. Now all he needed was some time.

Suddenly he heard a loud, bloodcurdling scream coming from the library.

It wasn't a human scream, though.

The scream came from a vampire.

CHAPTER Eight

Drak rushed down the stairs. Why hadn't he told his friends to go home when the Chompulas showed up? He should never have trusted those blood-sucking vultures.

He burst into the library, prepared for the worst. Everyone was clustered together in a small circle by the fireplace. The candles had all been blown out. The room felt dark and spooky.

Drak could tell by the expressions on his friends' faces that something awful had happened. Chris looked like he was about to cry, and Steven was hanging onto Brendan's arm.

Then Drak noticed Uncle Mort. He had a giant smirk on his face. So did Aunt Esther, sitting beside him. Drak narrowed his eyes. Cannibals!

Drak angrily pushed his way to the center of the circle. "I'm really sorry, guys," he said to his friends. "This is all my fault."

Drak's eyes dropped to the floor. He gasped. There sat Doug in the center in a lifeless heap. Poor Doug. His head leaned back. His eyes were closed. His mouth hung open.

Drak turned angrily to Uncle Mort. "I can't believe you would do this to the funniest kid in the third grade."

Doug opened his eyes. "Do you mind?" he said. "I'm in the middle of a ghost story."

Drak jumped back. "Doug! You're alive!"

"Of course I'm alive. I'm telling a ghost story."

"Drak, move," said Steven. "You're in my way."

Drak slowly stared at the faces around him. Ella and Margaret were clutching each other too. Jeremy had covered his ears.

Drak peeked at the back of Doug's neck. Not a single tooth mark.

Relieved, he crept back to a place in the circle.

Doug leaned forward. In a hushed voice he said, "And then the hunter told the old man that he had chopped off the werewolf's hand and he had it in his bag. 'Would you like to see it?' he asked the old man. The hunter opened the bag and pulled out the hand. The man screamed. It was his own wife's hand. He recognized her wedding ring."

No one said a word. Then Margaret started crying. "I didn't like that story," she said. "It was too scary."

"Way too scary," said Ella.

Doug lifted his eyebrows up and down. "That's the whole point."

"I kinda liked it," said Jeremy.

"Me too," said Chris.

Margaret gave him a dirty look.

"Mom," said Vincent in a whiny voice. "My finger hurts where it got shut in the coffin."

"And my head hurts where I banged it on the floor," said Margaret.

"You should see my foot," said Ella. "It's more swollen than your dumb head."

"There, there," said Aunt Esther.

Ella stood up and limped toward the fireplace. "I'm getting hungry."

Drak checked the grandfather clock in the corner. He crossed his fingers and hoped his timing was right. "Who's ready to eat?"

"Me!" screamed Vincent.

"Me!" shouted Steven.

"Then follow me to the kitchen," said Drak. Everyone rushed for the door. "Hold your horses," said Drak.

He barely beat his guests to the kitchen table. Mrs. Fangula had already put out several pitchers of blood for the Chompulas and sodas for the humans.

"Yum! Cherry juice," said Steven, reaching for the blood.

Drak grabbed the pitcher out of Steven's hands just in time. "That's not for you," he said.

"Why? What is it?" asked Steven.

"Um . . . " Drak didn't want to scare his guests. "It's for them," he said, motioning toward the Chompulas. He lowered his voice. "They're on a special liquid diet."

Steven stared at the Chompulas. "Even the skinny ones?" he whispered back.

Drak nodded. "It's something that runs in the family."

"Oh," said Steven. "Thanks for telling me."

Drak smiled. "No problem." He shoved the pitcher toward the Chompulas, who'd already polished off the other two.

Jeremy glanced around. "So where's *our* food?"

The doorbell rang. Drak smiled at his mother. "Coming right up," he said.

Drak ran out to answer the door.

Moments later he returned to the kitchen, carrying two large white cardboard boxes. He held them as far away from his body as he could.

"Dig in," he said, tossing the boxes onto the table.

"What is it?" asked Jeremy.

"Pizza!" said Drak. "Two large pepperonis with extra garlic." He ran to the far side of the room to escape the fumes.

"Garlic!" Uncle Mort sputtered. "Get me out of here!" He stood up so fast he knocked over his chair.

The Chompulas fled the table and joined Drak and his mother by the window.

"What's with them?" asked Doug.

Uncle Mort was steamed. "Garlic!" he screamed, shaking his fist at Drak. "How dare you spoil the taste of all that delightful fresh blood with *garlic*? Have you no sense at all?"

Aunt Esther fanned the air. "This is terrible," [illegible] muttered. "Really awful."

[illegible] grinned at his mother, who had covered [illegible] th her hand. Vampires hate garlic. [illegible] an't stand it.

"How's the pizza, guys?" asked Drak, breathing through his mouth.

"Great! Why aren't you eating, Drak?" said Brendan."

"I'm still full from dinner," said Drak.

"You're missing great pizza," said Steven, helping himself to another slice. "Sure you don't want any?"

Drak pulled his T-shirt up over his nose. "Positive."

Vincent whimpered beside Drak. "I want to go home, Dad," he said, pinching his nose. "I can't breathe, and my finger hurts."

"Me too," said Margaret. "I'm not having any fun here. All I can think about is that werewolf's hand. And it stinks in here."

"You're right. We're leaving," Uncle Mort announced. "That garlic has ruined my appetite."

Drak's mother smiled. "Oh, I'm so sorry. If you'd like, I can pack up the rest of that blood for you. You might get hungry again on your way home."

"No, thanks," said Aunt Esther in a huffy voice. "We've had enough."

The Chompulas quickly got their things together. They didn't even bother to say goodbye to Drak's friends.

SURF
DOGGIE

"Vlad will be sorry to have missed you," Drak's mother said as Aunt Esther climbed into the car.

"Hmph," she said, slamming the door. The car screeched off.

Drak and his mother went back to the kitchen. Drak's friends had lit his birthday cake. "Happy Birthday to you," they sang. When the song was over, Drak blew out the candles and cut the cake. He even tried a little bite. It tasted awful, but the others seemed to like it.

Jeremy came in carrying Drak's birthday presents. "This is the best part, opening the presents," he said, piling them up on the table.

Drak opened them one by one. Chris got him a soccer ball, Brendan gave him another Surf Doggies T-shirt, Doug got him a rock kit (Drak wasn't sure what it was until Jeremy explained), Steven got him a book ("My mother picked it out," he said), and Jeremy got him a baseball glove and a new pair of surfer sunglasses with mirror lenses.

"Oh, good," said Doug when Drak tried on the sunglasses. "Now I can check out my hair without having to go to the boys' room."

Everyone laughed.

"This is the coolest party I've ever been to," said Chris. "All who agree say aye."

"Aye," they all said.

Drak grinned. Even he had to say that his slumber party had turned out better than he could have ever imagined.